D0501159

The King & the Three Thieves

A • PERSIAN • TALE

RETOLD AND ILLUSTRATED BY

Kristen Balouch

VIKING

King Abbas was a real king of Persia (1587–1629), and he really had a long, magnificent moustache. He was curious about the common people. So curious, in fact, that he may have even disguised himself as a poor man and slipped out of his palace to meet them. The common people liked the king. They liked him so much that they told their children stories about him. When my husband was a boy in Iran this story of King Abbas was passed on to him by his father. —K. B.

Thank you to Omid and Baba Majeed for passing this story on, to Cathy and Denise for their expert direction, and to my family and friends for sharing their wonderful insights.

VIKING
Published by the Penguin Group
Penguin Putnam Books for Young Readers,
345 Hudson Street, New York, New York 10014, U.S.A.

Penguin Books Ltd, Registered Offices: Harmondsworth, Middlesex, England

First published in 2000 by Viking,
a division of Penguin Putnam Books for Young Readers.

10 9 8 7 6 5 4 3 2 1

Copyright © Kristen Balouch, 2000
All rights reserved

LIBRARY OF CONGRESS CATALOGING-IN-PUBLICATION DATA
Balouch, Kristen.
The king & three thieves : a Persian tale / retold and illustrated by Kristen Balouch.
p. cm.
Summary: King Abbas appears to get caught up in the schemes of three thieves but he has a few tricks of his own and ultimately saves his kingdom from starvation.
ISBN 0-670-88059-0 (hardcover)
[1. Fairy tales. 2. Folklore—Iran.] I. Title: King and three thieves. II. Title.
PZ8.B215 Ki 2000 398.2'0955—dc21 00-008764

Printed in Hong Kong
Set in ClearfaceGothic

The illustrations were created on a Macintosh computer using Adobe Illustrator software, and were inspired by Iranian pottery from Nishapur.

FOR BAILEY AND AUDEN

Long ago in the faraway land of Persia there lived a king with a long, magnificent moustache. His name was King Abbas and he loved to eat. Every night he ate extravagant dinners, but every night he ate alone.

One evening the king sat down to a dinner of fish with pomegranates over saffron rice. But when he tried to pick up the fish, it began to hop around the dish. The king could not eat his dinner, so he sent for his trusted counselor, the vizier.

The vizier looked at the fish. "Your majesty, it is a sign. There are hungry people in your kingdom. Feed them and then you will be able to eat your dinner."

King Abbas wrapped up some food, disguised himself as a poor man, and slipped out of the palace.

He searched through his kingdom until he came upon three men in ragged clothes whispering around a fire.

The first man had red round lips. The second had brilliant eyes, and the third had a tremendous nose.

The king shared his dinner with the three hungry men. After dinner, as they relaxed around the fire, the men shared their secret with the king.

"We are going to rob the king," they confided.

"Impossible!" exclaimed the king.

"Not with our special powers," the first thief whispered through red round lips. "I can whistle a tune that will put anyone to sleep."

The second thief looked at the king with his brilliant eyes. "I can see through walls."

The third thief sniffed with his tremendous nose. "My sneeze is so strong it can blow a door right off its hinges."

The king looked at the first thief's lips, the second thief's eyes, and the third thief's nose. As he twirled his moustache he said, "I have a power too. If you are caught I will free you with a mere twitch of my moustache."

The king's moustache looked magnificent, so the thieves invited him along.

The king and the three thieves stole swiftly through the night.

When they reached the palace the first thief went up to the gate, pursed his round lips, and whistled a soft *woooooo hooooooo*. The air became still and heavy. All the guards fell into a deep sleep and slowly sank to the ground. The first thief waved for the others to join him. The king stared at his sleeping guards in disbelief.

The second thief looked in each direction, then led them through a maze of odd little doors until they came to a beautiful mosaic door. The king was amazed. The thieves had actually found his treasury.

The third thief motioned to the others to stand back. His nose started to tremble and quiver. *Aaaaaaah choooooo!* He sneezed a great sneeze. It blew the great door right off its hinges! The king was stunned.

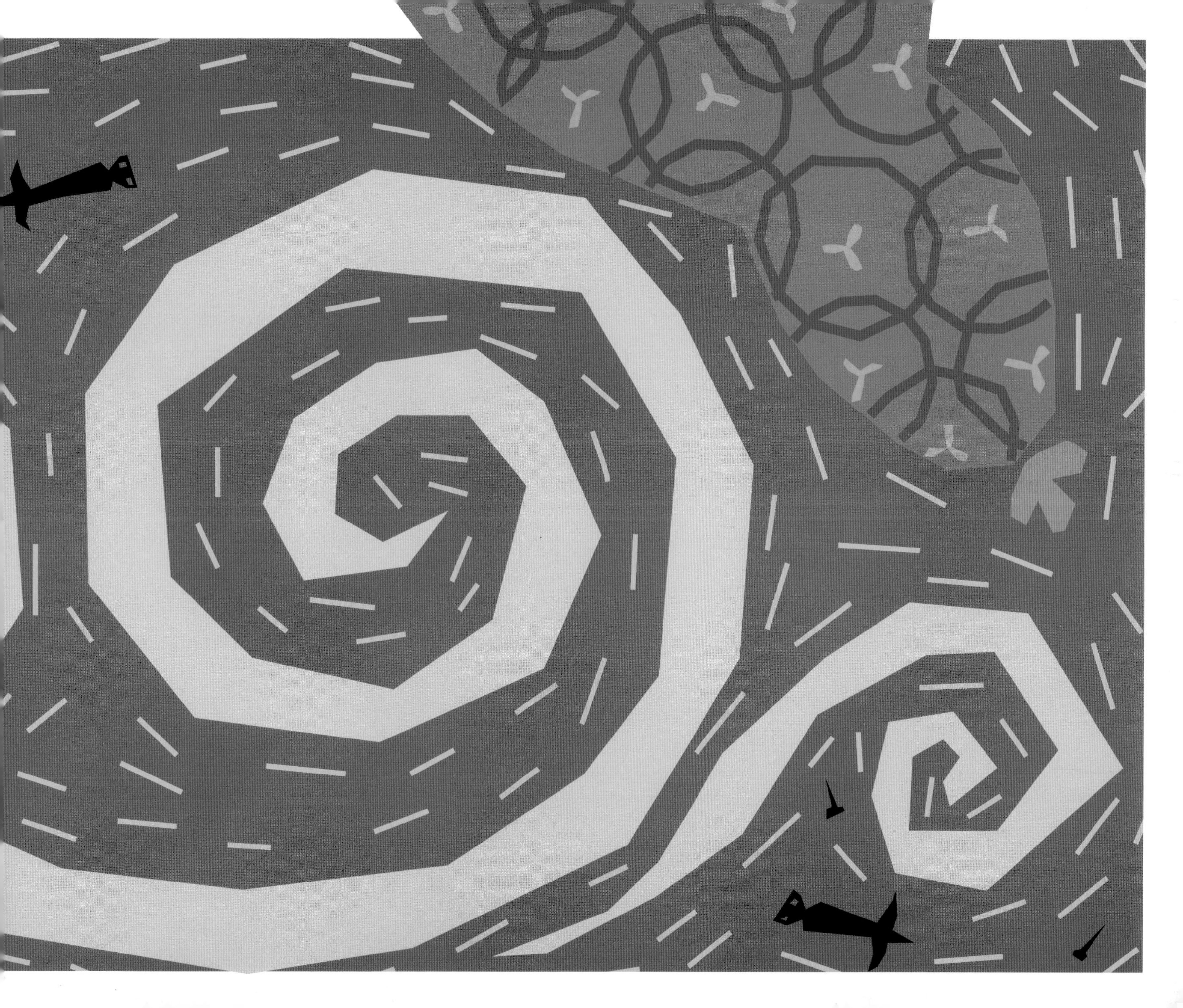

Before them stood a brilliant chamber full of magnificent treasures. The thieves giggled with joy as they stuffed their sacks with sparkling gems and shiny gold coins. Then they placed the door back on its hinges and crept out of the palace with the bewildered king trailing behind them.

Back around the fire the thieves shared their stolen treasure with the king.

The king waited for the three thieves to fall asleep, and then he slipped away and returned to his palace.

The king put on his royal robes, woke up his sleeping guards, and ordered them to arrest the thieves. Soon the king's guards were dragging the thieves across the square, through the palace, into the crowded court.

The king sent for his vizier.

The vizier looked over the three thieves. "Your Majesty, they are a sign. Power can be used for evil or for good."

The king looked sternly at the vizier. "These men are thieves." And he marched up to his throne.

The great Persian king looked down at the frightened thieves. “So you thought you could rob the king!” he bellowed.

The three thieves pleaded their innocence.

King Abbas threw off his royal robes, revealing the ragged clothes underneath. The court gasped. The thieves begged to be forgiven.

But the king just beckoned his guards.

"Take these three to the dungeon!"

The guards surrounded the thieves. The first thief nudged the second thief. The second thief nudged the third. The third thief gathered his wits and called out, "Your Majesty, last night you said if we were caught a twitch of your moustache would free us. Please twitch your moustache now."

The king paused. The guards stopped. The court was silent.

The king thought. He looked at the first thief's lips, the second thief's eyes, and the third thief's nose. Then the king thought some more. He looked at his vizier and remembered what he had said. "Power can be used for good or for evil." Slowly a smile spread across the king's face and then his moustache began to twitch.

At last the king declared, "A king never breaks his promise. All three of you shall live in the palace. Together we will use our powers to make sure that no one in the kingdom ever goes hungry again."

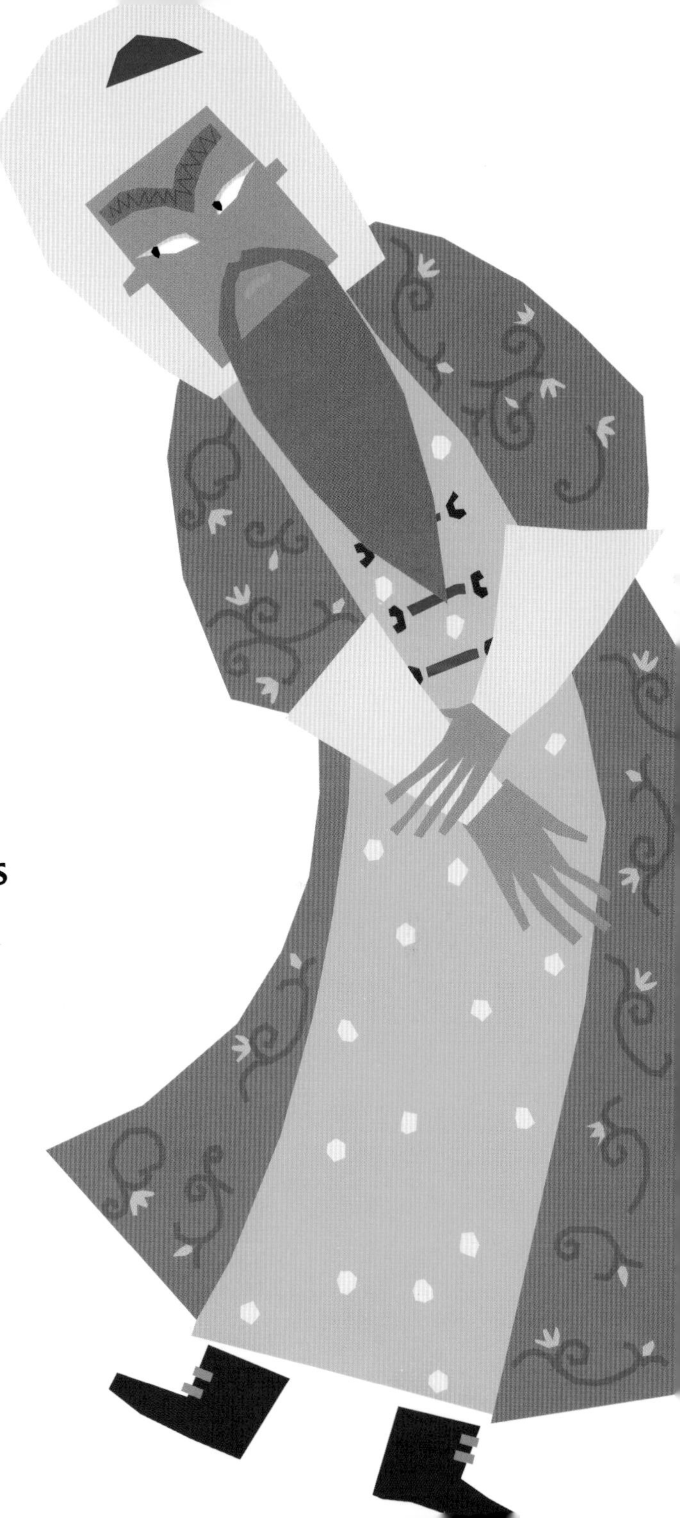

The three were so grateful that the first thief's round lips broke into a wide smile, the second thief's eyes beamed with happiness, and the third thief's nose tingled with delight. The court cheered their kind and wise king. And the vizier looked to the king and gave a silent nod.

From that day on the king never ate dinner alone. The king's guards, his trusted vizier, and the three men all ate dinner with the king. And whenever they ate fish with pomegranates over saffron rice, the king would smile.